Billy's Big Game

	DATE DUE	
JUN 0 9 2009	DEC 10 2010	
MAY 2 2 2010	AUG 1 3 2011	
JUL 2 9 2010		
MAR 3 1 2011	SEP 0 9 2011	
	JUN 1 3 2012	

ISBN 0-7696-4177-6

50395

EAN

9 780769 641775

School Specialty
Publishing

Text Copyright © Evans Brothers Ltd. 2005. Illustration copyright ©
Evans Brothers Ltd. 2005. First published by Evans Brothers Limited, 2A
Portman Mansions, Chiltern Street, London W1U 6NR, United
Kingdom. This edition published under license from Zero to Ten
Limited. All rights reserved. Printed in China. This edition published in
2005 by Gingham Dog Press, an imprint of School Specialty Publishing,
a member of the School Specialty Family.

Library of Congress-in-Publication Data is on file with the publisher.

Send all inquiries to:
School Specialty Publishing
8720 Orion Place
Columbus, OH 43240-2111

ISBN 0-7696-4177-6

1 2 3 4 5 6 7 8 9 10 EVN 10 09 08 07 06 05

Billy's Big Game

By Paul Harrison

Illustrated by Silvia Raga

GINGHAM DOG
PRESS

Columbus, Ohio

Today is the big game.

Billy is with his team.

Everybody is there.

9

The game begins.

11

Billy heads the ball.

He gets fouled.

Yellow card!

Billy has the ball again.

He shoots.

21

He scores.

23

He wins the game!

Billy gets the trophy.

He lifts it high…

and wakes up!

Words I Know

game	card
team	scores
shoots	wins
ball	wakes

Think About It!

1. What kind of game did Billy play?

2. What is a yellow card?

3. Why was Billy's shot important?

4. Did this really happen? How do you know?

The Story and You

1. Do you play a game or sport? What is it?

2. Did you ever score the winning point? How did you feel?

3. If you could be a sports hero, who would you be?